I, *Geronimo Stilton*, hav lot of mouse friends, but no
spooky as my friend CREEP
VON CACKLEFUR! She is an
enchanting and MYSTERIOUS mouse with
a pet bat named **Bitewing**. Creepella lives in a
CEMETERY, sleeps in a marble **sarcophagus**, and drives
a **hearse**. By night she is a special effects and set
designer for SCARY FILMS, and by day she's studying
to become a journalist! Her father, Boris von
Cacklefur, runs the funeral home Fabumouse
Funerals, and the von Cacklefur family owns the
CREEPY Cacklefur Castle, which sits on top of a
skull-shaped mountain in MYSTERIOUS VALLEY.

YIKES! I'm a real 'fraidy
mouse, but even I think
Creepella and her family are
AWFULLY fascinating.
I can't wait for you to read
this **fa-mouse-ly funny** and
SPECTACULARLY SPOOKY tale!

Geronimo Stilton

Creepella von Cacklefur

Bitewing

Grandpa Frankenstein

Billy Squeakspeare

An extremely mad scientist and an expert in Egyptian mummies.

A journalist who lives in Mysterious Valley and solves spooky cases with her inseparable pet bat, Bitewing.

A famous writer and friend of Creepella.

Shivereen

Grandma Crypt

Snip and Snap

Troublemaking twins and expert spies.

Creepella's favorite niece.

Dolores

Kafka

She loves spiders, and her pet is a gigantic tarantula named Dolores.

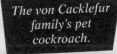

The von Cacklefur family's pet cockroach.

Booey the Poltergeist

The mischievous ghost who haunts Cacklefur Castle.

Boneham

The butler to the von Cacklefur family, and a snob right down to the tips of his whiskers.

Baby

He was adopted and raised with love by the von Cacklefurs.

Madame LaTomb

The family housekeeper. A ferocious were-canary nests in her hair.

Chef Stewrat

The cook at Cacklefur Castle. He dreams of creating the ultimate stew.

Boris von Cacklefur

Creepella's father, and the funeral director at Fabumouse Funerals.

Chompers

The von Cacklefur family's meat-eating guard plant.

Geronimo Stilton

CREEPELLA VON CACKLEFUR

THE THIRTEEN GHOSTS

Scholastic Inc.

New York   Toronto   London   Auckland
Sydney   Mexico City   New Delhi   Hong Kong

ISBN 978-0-545-30742-0

Published by Scholastic Inc., 557 Broadway, New York, NY 10012.

Text by Geronimo Stilton
Original title *Tredici fantasmi per Tenebrosa*
Cover by Giuseppe Ferrario
Illustrations by Ivan Bigarella (pencils) and Giorgio Campioni (color)
Map of Cacklefur Castle: Color by Christian Aliprandi
Graphics by Yuko Egusa

Special thanks to Tracey West
Translated by Emily Clement
Interior design by Kay Petronio

20 19 18 17   17 18 19 20/0

Printed in the U.S.A.   40
First printing, August 2011

A MYSTERIOUS MESSAGE

Night fell on New Mouse City as quickly as a flash of lightning. The sky was as black as the eyes of a hungry cat. Only the **CHEDDAR YELLOW** light of the full moon **shone** through the **DARKNESS**. I pulled my jacket closer and hurried on my way.

Sorry, I haven't introduced myself. My name is Stilton, *Geronimo Stilton*. I am the publisher of The Rodent's Gazette, the most **famouse** newspaper on Mouse Island!

You're probably wondering: What was a

mouse like me doing out on a **spooky** night like this? Well, I'll tell you.

You see, I had to go back to my office to get some papers. I had done a bunch of research on **SCARY** stories. Just thinking about those stories makes my whiskers curl with fright!

Anyway, when I arrived at The Rodent's Gazette, I jumped in surprise. A light was **glowing** in one of the windows. I thought that was **STRANGE**. I'm always careful to turn the lights off when I leave. I don't like wasting energy!

I **slowly** stepped inside my office. **Whoosh!** A gust of **ICY** wind blew through an open window. I didn't remember leaving a window open. I went to close it when . . .

"**AAAHH!!!**"

I noticed a purple **BAT** sitting on the windowsill, **STARING** at me!

I let out another scream of **TERROR** and fainted.

I started to wake up when I felt something tickling my whiskers. The bat was waving a wing in front of my nose.

"What are you **fainting** for?" the bat screeched in my ear.

"Wake up! Wake up! Wake up! Message for you! Message for you! Message for you!"

I was terrified. "F-f-f-from wh-whom?" I stammered.

The bat sneered. "Why, from CREEPELLA VON CACKLEFUR, of course!"

That's when I finally recognized him: It was **Bitewing**, the strange

von Cacklefur family's pet bat.

Then I noticed that Bitewing was holding a sealed roll of papers in his **claws**. Before I could ask what it was, he dropped it on my desk and flew off into the DARK night, squealing,

"Publish it! No complaints! That's an order!"

I must admit that I was relieved to see **Bitewing** fly off. I took a deep breath to calm myself. Then I sat down at my desk. With trembling paws, I unrolled the papers and began to read.

My friend CREEPELLA VON CACKLEFUR had written a long story set in the faraway **MYSTERIOUS VALLEY**. After reading just a few lines, I could tell I was in for a chilling adventure.

CREEPELLA had drawn illustrations to go along with the story. I have to say, she has a very ORIGINAL style!

The story was so fascinating that I couldn't put it down. I read all through the night. I finally finished when the first RAYS OF SUN shone through my office window.

I yawned. "What a strange tale."

At that moment, my nephew **Benjamin** and his friend **Bugsy Wugsy** walked into my office.

"Hey, Uncle, what are you reading?" Benjamin asked curiously.

I read them one of my favorite sections of the story. They loved it!

"It's such a STRANGE story . . . but THRILLING!" they both agreed.

My sister, THEA, arrived next. She works as a special correspondent for The Rodent's Gazette. I showed her the story, too.

"These illustrations are STRANGE . . . but THRILLING!" Thea commented.

Then my cousin TRAP stumbled into my office. He read the story while eating a cheese sandwich, smearing mozzarella all over my desk.

"It's a STRANGE adventure . . . but THRILLING!" Trap said.

One by one, all of the mice who work at The Rodent's Gazette came into my office. They were curious to see what all the fuss was about. I shared

Creepella's story and illustrations with all of them.

"What **STRANGE** characters . . . but so **THRILLING!**" they murmured. Soon my office was crowded with chatting mice. The last time I saw everyone so excited was on **FREE CHEESE DAY** at the market! Then a loud voice rang through my office.

"GRAAAAAAANDSON!"

Strange...
but thrilling!

Strange...
but thrilling!

Strange...
but thrilling!

Strange...
but thrilling!

Strange...
but thrilling!

It was my grandfather, **William Shortpaws**.

"What's happening here? Is this some kind of *party*?" he yelled.

"Let me tell you —" I began.

"I have no time for stories," he **SNAPPED**. "Get to work!"

"But this *is* a story. I mean, a story is the reason we're excited," I explained. I handed him Creepella's tale. "What do you think? Isn't it **STRANGE**?"

Strange... but thrilling!

Strange... but thrilling!

Strange... but thrilling!

Strange... but thrilling!

Strange... but thrilling!

He read the pages, tapping his foot on the floor. His tail **twitched**. He stroked his **whiskers**. Finally, he shouted, "It's an **EXTREMELY STRANGE** story, Grandson . . . but it's also **EXTREMELY THRILLING!**"

As you can see, everyone was very excited about Creepella's story. So I decided to publish it! It's called **THE THIRTEEN GHOSTS**. In fact, it's the very story you hold in your paws.

HAPPY READING!

Strange . . . but very thrilling! Now back to work!

THE THIRTEEN GHOSTS

Story and Illustrations by
Creepella von Cacklefur

GOOD MORNING, GLOOMERIA!

Deep in the dark heart of Mysterious Valley lay the ancient city of **Gloomeria**. Still wrapped in the **shadows** of night, the city was as dreary as ever. A thick **FOG** floated through the streets like a ghost, pushed by a breath of wind fainter than a **mummy's** sigh.

The people of Gloomeria still **SNORED** in their beds.

Only a few sneaky shadows moved through the dark streets: the **bats** from the valley. They zipped and zoomed around before going home for the day. As they soared and swirled, the first light of dawn began to shine. A sharp squeal rang through the valley.

"Good morning, Gloomeria!"

The squealer was a small purple bat named **Bitewing** with pointy teeth and BRIGHT yellow eyes. Bitewing flew CROOKEDLY from one roof to the next. He bounced from chimney to chimney like a ball in a pinball machine. He was lost in the FOG! He flapped his wings.

FLAP! FLAP! FLAP!

As he zigzagged, he mumbled to himself, "This F○G is so thick, I can't see my wing in front of my face!"

Finally, he let out a happy SHRIEK.

"Home! Home! Home!"

He heard the familiar notes of a pipe organ **FAR, FAR AWAY** in the fog.

Then he flew toward the sound, beating his wings against the *wind*.

Bitewing

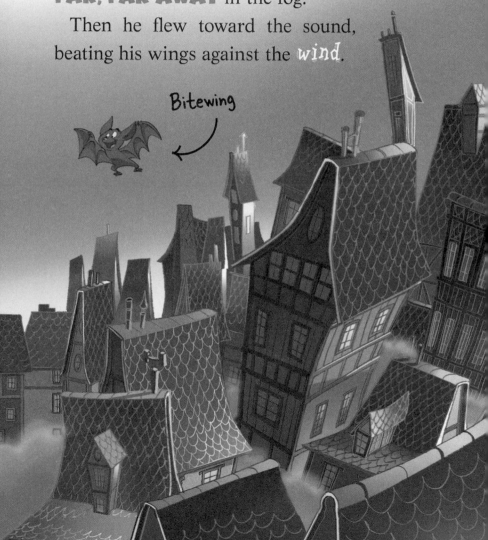

He flew away from the city, toward an eerie hill shaped like a SKULL. A spooky castle sat on top of the hill: **Cacklefur Castle**! It was the STRANGE home of the STRANGEST family in the very STRANGE Mysterious Valley — the von Cacklefur family!

Bitewing flew to a window at the top of the castle. Through the glass he heard the

A voice from inside called out, "**Bitewing**, you're finally HOME! Come here!"

The face of a **bewitching** young mouse appeared at the window. She had JET-BLACK hair and deep green eyes.

CACKLEFUR CASTLE

Beware of Monster!

It was CREEPELLA VON CACKLEFUR, a journalist who was always on the hunt for the most mysterious stories. The music that had helped Bitewing find his way home was Creepella's creepy alarm clock.

CREEPELLA tossed a tasty treat to her bat. It was Bug-flavored candy, his favorite! Bitewing squeaked with happiness.

"Thank you! Thank you! Thank you! Yummy! Yum! Yummmmmm!"

Creepella looked out at the dismal valley in front of her and sighed. "I must get to work. I have to write a truly CHILLING article for *THE SHIVERY NEWS*."

Every creature in Mysterious Valley read **THE SHIVERY NEWS**.

"I already have the title," Creepella continued. "'**The Secret Life of the Ghosts of Mysterious Valley.**'"

Bitewing fluttered around the room. "The title's not bad, but if you don't **HURRY UP** and write the article, you'll never make the deadline!" he squeaked.

"Well, I have to research it first!" Creepella replied, annoyed. "I'm a serious journalist, after all!"

Bitewing giggled. "**Hee hee hee!** If you're such a serious journalist, you should be using the right tools!"

He **DOVE** into an old, dusty trunk. Huffing and puffing, he pulled out an old typewriter.

"This belonged to your great-

great-grandmother Misery von Cacklefur, the famous author of **HORROR** novels," the bat explained.

"You're so **OLD-FASHIONED**, Bitewing," Creepella scoffed. "Don't you know that everyone uses COMPUTERS now? Even Misery wouldn't use that old thing if she were alive today."

Her green eyes gleamed. "What I really need is the right **OUTFIT**! Let me get ready. We can talk more when I'm done."

"Of course!" Bitewing agreed. "How can you write anything if you're not properly **dressed**?"

GHOSTLY GLAMOUR

Creepella put on her **makeup** in front of the bathroom mirror.

"It would be best if I could meet a lot of GHOSTS," she murmured. "Then I could ask them what everyone wants to know: 'What are your favorite houses to **HAUNT**?' 'What is your secret to being **scary**?' Then my article would be truly chilling!"

She brushed her long **BLACK HAIR**. Then she styled it with a rotting green GEL made from spiderwebs. Finally, she brushed her cheeks with POWDER the color of the full moon.

"Perfect! Now I look pale and ghostly!" She looked at herself in the mirror, satisfied.

Then she took her favorite PERFUME and sprayed it behind her ears.

"The scent of lizard spit! What a wonderful STENCH!" she exclaimed. "Now I just need one last GLOOMY touch."

She carefully applied her favorite lip gloss: **Dismal Drool**.

She looked at herself in her large mirror.

"You look gorgeous, Miss Creepella!" the mirror said in a high-pitched voice.

"Thanks, Mirror!" CREEPELLA replied. "Now I just have to pick the right dress."

Next Creepella turned to **Wardrobe**, the huge walking, talking cabinet that held all of her clothes.

"**Wardrobe!**" she called. "Are you ready? It's an important day and I need to look extra GLOOMY."

Wardrobe opened its doors as *quickly* as a bat flaps its wings. "Here are my suggestions, Miss Creepella! Today is a lovely FOGGY day. It's **SIXTY** degrees out, with 99 percent humidity. I suggest outfit number 368: a **long** purple dress. It has just the right amount of GLOOM about it. I'd finish the look with a pink jacket made of the finest COBWEBS, perfect for a beautifully **HUMID** day like today. I'd also recommend a set of imitation **WEREWOLF-SKIN** gloves. And if you have an important meeting, you must wear your **SILKY** bat-wing shawl."

"Thank you, thank you, **Wardrobe**," Creepella said gratefully. "You always know just what to recommend. Today I don't have any meetings. I just need to find some fabulously **frightening** ideas!"

She put on the purple dress. Then she opened her jewelry box and put a *spider* necklace around her neck.

Wardrobe

Many legends surround this antique wardrobe, which once belonged to Creepella's great-great-great-grandmother, Chi-Chi von Cacklefur. Chi-Chi was the most famous fashionista in Mysterious Valley. The stories say that there are secret passageways, trapdoors, and trunks that Wardrobe opens only on special occasions, such as the Whirling Bat Ball. No one knows how big it is, or how many outfits it holds.

Coat for the Grand Spider Ball

Full Moon glasses

Halloween hat

Swamp Stench perfume

Forgotten jewelry box

Creepella **SIGHED**, sat down at her computer, and began to write.

Sensational article by Creepella von Cacklefur (to be read only by those who don't suffer from shivers, frights, *and* **terrors**!*)*

"First of all, what does it mean to be a ghost?" she asked herself.

She walked over to the bookcase and took out an enormous book:

DAILY ALMANAC OF MYSTERIOUS VALLEY, WITH CHAPTERS ON THE FULL MOON, ECLIPSES, AND GHOSTLY BEHAVIOR

CREEPELLA flipped through the MOLDY pages.

"Aha!" she exclaimed. "Haunted castles . . . prankster ghosts . . . mysterious events. This is just what I need to write my article!"

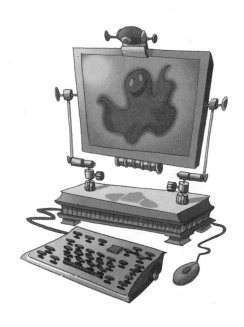

Do Not Disturb!

Creepella wrote a few lines. Then she stopped and **STARED** at the ceiling. She **STARED** out the window, and then **STARED** at the floor. Finally, she burst out, "TOADSTOOLS! I need some inspiration!"

"I bet I could write it as quickly as I can flap my wing!" Bitewing teased.

CREEPELLA stood up. "That's enough! Shoo! SCRAM!"

She waved away **Bitewing**, who made a fast exit through the door. Then she hung a  on the doorknob:

DO NOT DISTURB!
(No matter what!)
I am writing an article.
No visitors allowed, including bats, cockroaches, mummies, werewolves, etc.

—Creepella von Cacklefur

She had just closed the door when someone **knocked** and came in. It was Boneham, the von Cacklefur family's butler.

"Miss Creepella, I must inform you that **breakfast** is served!" the butler said.

"I have an article to write!" Creepella told him. "I don't want to be **disturbed** today, and I am not coming down for breakfast!"

Boneham raised an eyebrow,

What is it?

but he didn't leave. Seconds later, someone else **knocked** on the door. A mouse with a **WERE-CANARY** in her hair walked in.

It was **Madame LaTomb**, the family housekeeper. She was very concerned.

"**CREEPELLA**, my dear, why are you skipping breakfast?" she asked. "You know that an **earthworm** smoothie is the best way to start the day!"

Breakfast is served!

Madame LaTomb

"Yes, but I need to write," Creepella insisted.

She started to close the door, but two more mice stepped in. Now she was **face-to-face** with her father, Boris von Cacklefur, and Grandma Crypt. Their whiskers were twitching with worry.

"Creepella, are you okay?" her father asked. "Does your throat **HURT**, or your head, or your feet, or your back, or your tummy, or your —"

Boris von Cacklefur

Grandma Crypt

Creepella interrupted him. "Thanks, but I'm F-I-N-E. There's nothing **wrong**!"

Suddenly, they heard strange noises. It sounded like someone was chewing on the doorknob:

ChOmp!
ChOmp!

It was CHOMPERS, the von Cacklefur family's meat-eating plant.

Chompers

"Chompers, get your teeth off of my doorknob!" Creepella scolded. "You'll scratch it!"

A big red COCKROACH crawled out from behind the plant. It dragged a cookie behind it.

The cockroach offered the cookie to Creepella.

Creepella sighed. "Thanks, **Kafka**, you're sweet. But I don't want your cookies for breakfast!"

Knock! Knock! Knock!

"Who is it now?" Creepella asked.

The door opened and in came CHEF STEWRAT, the family cook, dragging a big pot of stew.

"Miss Creepella, please tell me the truth!" CHEF STEWRAT looked very upset. "Are you skipping breakfast because you **hate** my stew? Where did I go wrong? I could add a nice stinky **sock** for more flavor. Or a little piece of dragon **BONE**. Or maybe some **earthworm** spleen. Tell me the problem, and I'll fix it!"

The chef started to cry, and Creepella tried to make him feel better. "CHEF STEWRAT, your stew is DELICIOUS as always," she began. "It's just that . . ."

Chef Stewrat blew his nose and then threw his handkerchief into the pot. "SNIFF! You're just saying that to make me feel better. But I know that you don't like my stew anymore. I'll never cook again!"

Shivereen, Creepella's niece, whispered in her ear. "Auntie, look how sad CHEF STEWRAT is," Shivereen said. "Please come downstairs and have breakfast!"

CREEPELLA gave in. "All right, I'll have breakfast!"

Breakfast wouldn't help with her article, but at least

Shivereen

The terrible twins,
Snip and Snap

Chef
Stewrat

Chef Stewrat's
famouse stew

Chef Stewrat was smiling again.

They all went down to the dining room. The terrible twins, Snip and Snap, were already seated at the table. When they saw Creepella come in, they both shouted, "Sit here next to us!"

Creepella sighed. "I know you two — you've probably covered the chair with STINKY wild lavender oil, or some other flowery scent. Yuck!"

The twins were disappointed. "We never get to play PRANKS on you," they complained. "You always figure them out!"

Creepella chose another seat and quickly ate her breakfast. "I need to write my article in peace," she muttered to herself. "I'll have to go to the only quiet place in the castle. . . ."

GRANDPA FRANKENSTEIN'S STUDY

After breakfast, CREEPELLA left the dining room. She walked down a long hallway, turned right, and opened a squeaky door. She passed through a crypt. Then she walked down a narrow staircase, ducking to avoid the spiders hanging from the ceiling. Finally, she stopped in front of a door with a sign on it:

GRANDPA FRANKENSTEIN'S STUDY

KEEP OUT, OR I'LL TURN YOU INTO A MUMMY!

"**Grandpa**, it's me!" Creepella shouted. She opened the door and entered the **COFFIN-**shaped study. Dark purple velvet covered the walls, and the room was stuffed with all kinds of unusual **gadgets** and equipment.

Grandpa Frankenstein's green **snout** stuck up over a lab table in the back of the room. "Come in, my dearest granddaughter!" he called out in a shrill voice. "I'm over here, conducting an **EXPERIMENT**!"

Creepella was going to ask what kind of experiment it was, when . . . **bang**! A bright flash of **lightning** lit up the room. Creepella rushed over to her grandfather, worried.

"Grandpa, are you okay?" she asked.

"P-p-p-perfect!" he replied with a stutter.

Grandpa Frankenstein

His **FUR** was sticking straight up all over his body! But he was too **excited** to notice.

"Hurray! The experiment was a success! I have made **POWDERED** soup mix using mummy bandages," he said proudly. "I can see the headlines already: 'Prepare Authentic **MUMMY SOUP** in Your Own Kitchen!'"

He handed a cup of **SMOKING** soup to Creepella. "Would you like to taste it?

It tastes just like ancient **EGYPT**!"

"Um, thanks, Grandpa, but I just had breakfast," Creepella replied, shaking her head. "Anyway, I need your help! I have to write an article about ghosts, but I don't know where to start."

AAAP!

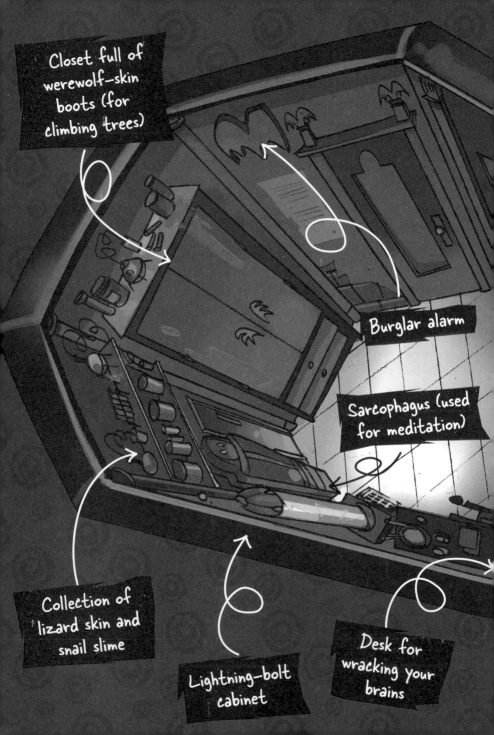

Booey

Grandpa Frankenstein **hugged** Creepella. "Of course I will help you, my dear granddaughter!" he cried.

"Thank you, Grandfather. You see, to write a truly CHILLING article, I need to interview a real ghost," Creepella explained.

Her grandfather thought for a moment. "Why don't you talk to Booey, the **GHOST** who haunts our castle?"

"I can't," CREEPELLA moaned. "Booey's on **vacation**.

HAPPY HAUNTING!

The Scottish ghosts say hello!
Booey

Creepella von Cacklefur
Cacklefur Castle
Gloomeria
Mysterious Valley

He's haunting an old Scottish castle. We just got a **POSTCARD** from him. Who knows when he's coming back!"

Grandpa Frankenstein thought some more. Then he smacked his paw on his forehead. "I've got it! My grandfather's grandfather's grandfather's grandfather used to say that Squeakspeare Mansion was **HAUNTED** by ghosts," he told her. "Do you know it? It's a deliciously **DREARY** mansion on the outskirts of **GLOOMERIA**. Why don't you check it out?"

Creepella hugged him. "Great idea, Grandpa. I'll go to Squeakspeare Mansion right now!"

GHOST GHOST GHOST GHOST GHOST GHOST GHOST GHOST GHOST GHOST GHOST GHOST GHOST GHOST GHOST GHOST

ON THE HUNT FOR A SCOOP

Creepella jumped into her car, a **TURBORAPID 3000**. The convertible **hearse** was the best one on the market.

Auntie, can I go with you?

Turborapid 3000

Shivereen ran after her. "Auntie, are you going after a Scoop? Can I go with you?"

"Of course!" CREEPELLA replied. "Bring the camera. You can be my official PHOTOGRAPHER!"

Bitewing fluttered past them, and Creepella caught him by the foot. "I need you to come, too, please. You can help me take notes!"

The purple bat sighed. "I was just going to take a nap!"

Shivereen and Bitewing strapped on their seat belts. Then Creepella drove down the long road leading away from Cacklefur Castle.

"Bitewing, you know every road in Mysterious Valley," Creepella said. "Which way to Squeakspeare Mansion?"

Bitewing looked around. "Let's see, Squeakspeare Mansion. First, drive down HAUNTED HILL. Then turn right on MUMMY ROAD."

"What's next?" Creepella asked.

"Cross the Bridge of Shaky Steps over the Whirling River," Bitewing instructed. "Now turn left on Ectoplasm Road. Squeakspeare Mansion is number thirteen!"

Then he started to hop in his seat.

"THAT'S IT! WE'RE HERE!"

Creepella stopped in front of a dark mansion with lots of TOWERS and balconies.

"Wow, this place is GHOULISH!" Bitewing squealed in excitement.

Creepella nodded. "The outside looks QUITE SPOOKY. I hope we find some ghosts inside!"

"I hope so, too!" Shivereen agreed. "But how are we going to get in?"

Suddenly, Bitewing's EYES lit up

SQUEAKSPEARE MANSION

with **surprise**. There's someone — or SOMETHING — moving in the garden!"

Shivereen looked over the rickety garden fence. "Bitewing's right, Auntie! There's a big pile of **suitcases** in there. I can see a *tail* sticking out from behind them. Maybe it's a ghost!"

With a nod, Creepella got out of the car and slowly crept up to the pile.

YANK! She gave the tail a good tug. "I've caught you, my dear ghost!" she shouted.

"Aaaaaaaaargh!"

a voice screamed.

A mouse
with **red**
hair appeared
from behind the
suitcases. He wasn't
SEE-THROUGH at all.

Creepella was disapointed.
"But you're not a GHOST!" she
complained.

Mysterious tail...

Bitewing **fluttered** around the mouse. "Confirmed! He is definitely not a ghost! He's a mouse from his **FUR** to his whiskers!"

The shaken-up mouse sat down on a suitcase. "**Bouncing bookmarks!** Wh-wh-who are you?" he asked, tenderly rubbing his tail.

"I'm Creepella von Cacklefur, and this is my niece Shivereen," Creepella replied. "Who are you?"

"My name is Squeakspeare, **BiLLy SQUEAKSPEARE**," the mouse responded.

"Marvelous!" Creepella cried happily. "Then you must be the owner of **Squeakspeare Mansion**. Can you let us in?"

"No, I can't . . . I mean, yes . . .

BILLY SQUEAKSPEARE

WHO IS HE? He is the famouse author of super-sappy romantic novels. His biggest bestseller is *Two Hearts and a Pot of Fondue*, a love story set in a cheese shop.

WHERE DOES HE LIVE? Billy just moved to a dark mansion on the edge of Gloomeria. He inherited the house from his great-great-great-uncle William. He hopes to find peace and quiet there so he can write his novels. But he doesn't know that things are never peaceful in Mysterious Valley. . . .

HOBBY: Growing roses to give to his girlfriend . . . if he ever gets one.

SECRET WISH: To star in a movie based on one of his novels, but it's only a wish. In real life, he's much too nervous to act in front of a camera!

FAVORITE FOOD: Ravioli (but only the kind filled with cheese) in a cheese sauce (but only if the cheese has been aged for twenty years) with chopped nuts (but only nuts from the trees that grow in Mousylvania).

No...I mean, yes!

I mean, who knows?" he stuttered.

"Is your tongue tied in a **KNOT** or something?" Creepella asked impatiently.

"No," Billy replied. "But I just inherited the mansion, and I haven't been able to get in myself!"

Creepella raised an eyebrow. "Don't you have the **KEYS**?"

Billy's whiskers were twitching nervously. "I do, but as soon as I step through the door, something pushes me back out! I end up flat on my fur with all four **paws** in the air."

"I smell a mystery!" Creepella exclaimed. "Are there any **CLUES**?"

BILLY took a piece of paper out of his pocket and gave it to Creepella. "I don't know about clues, but I do have this ⌐LETTER⌐.

To the distinguished Mr. Billy Squeakspeare:

At last we've found you! Where have you been hiding? We wish to inform you that you have inherited a mansion from your distant relative, William Squeakspeare. Squeakspeare Mansion is on the outskirts of Gloomeria, in the lovely (but of course, that's a matter of taste) Mysterious Valley.

We have enclosed the keys to the mansion, should you wish to live there (although you may change your mind!). We wish you the best of luck (you'll need it!).

Sincerely,

Gregor Ghastly, Esq.

P.S. I'm including a map of the house, but I wouldn't rely on it. The walls seem to be always moving!

P.P.S. If you have any trouble, don't ask us for help!

P.P.P.S. Could you send me an autographed copy of TWO HEARTS AND A POT OF FONDUE?

I received it a month ago from a lawyer in Mysterious Valley."

Shivereen clasped her PAWS together. "You wrote *Two Hearts and a Pot of Fondue*? That is a super-romantic novel! I've read it thirteen times!" she squealed.

"Why, yes, that's right. I'm a writer," Billy replied.

CREEPELLA wasn't impressed. She had her own article to worry about. "Good for you, Billy," she snapped. "Now let's stop wasting time."

"Yesss! We're hunting for ghosts!"

Bitewing added, flapping his wings.

Billy turned PALE. "Gh-gh-ghosts?" he stuttered.

"Yesss!" Bitewing squeaked. "We've heard that your house is FULL of them! They must be the ones who pushed you out the door."

"Let's go FIND them," Creepella said, impatiently tapping her paw.

Billy tried to **PROTEST**. "Do we have to? I mean, really . . ."

But it was no use. Creepella took him by the arm and **DRAGGED** him up to the front door. Shivereen and Bitewing followed behind.

"Billy, dear, please open the door,"

she said firmly. "If we go in together, they won't be able to push all of us out!"

SQUEAKSPEARE MANSION

13 ECTOPLASM ROAD, GLOOMERIA, MYSTERIOUS VALLEY

This gloomy home was built in 1813 by the famouse architect Timothy Tombstone, a specialist in the design of cemeteries. With its frosted windows and twisted towers, it's considered to be a masterpiece.

In 1913, director Cecil B. DeMouse chose it as the location for the classic horror film, SCREAMS AT MIDNIGHT.

It has changed hands several times over the years. No one has ever lived there for very long. That's probably because it's haunted by ghosts.

Squeakspeare
Manision

BILLY opened the door with his **key**. Creepella went in first. A **MOLDY** stench tickled her **whiskers**. The room was as

DARK as a werewolf's fur. The only light came from three flickering candles.

Billy trembled like a leaf. He thought he saw curious EYES staring at him from every direction.

"D-d-d-o you think we're b-b-being watched?" he stammered.

Bitewing silently flew next to Billy and whispered in his ear,

"**Booooooooooooooo!**"

Billy jumped. "Help! What was that?"

Bitewing laughed. "It's just me, Silly Billy!"

Before they could take another step, **BiLLY** shrieked again. "Wh-who pulled my whiskers?"

"You just walked into some COBWEBS," Bitewing said with a giggle. (Being a bat, he had no trouble getting around in the dark.)

"Still," CREEPELLA said thoughtfully. "Something's not right. Those candles just went out."

"You're right!" Shivereen cried. "I bet a GHOST blew them out!"

"It was probably a GHOST who lit them in the first place," Bitewing pointed out.

BiLLY shuddered. "A GH-GHOST?" He looked terrified.

Creepella stayed calm. She walked to a door and opened it.

"Looks like the kitchen," she remarked.

A **teapot** was steaming on the kitchen table in the center of the room. Some teabags were sticking out of the lid: Mousylvania Moldy Morning Brew. Next to the teapot, someone had left a half-eaten triple **chocolate** cake covered in **icing**.

"Hmm. It looks like someone was just making a snack," Shivereen guessed.

"Yes, you're right. Someone just made a **SNACK**!" Bitewing squeaked.

"**JUMPING MUMMIES!**" Creepella exclaimed. "Billy, someone just made a **SNACK**! Can you believe it?"

"A **S-SNACK**? How t-terrifying!" Billy said, shivering.

"It's another **CLUE**!" Creepella said. "We must keep **exploring** the house. It's so deliciously gloomy. Don't you think so, **BiLLY**?"

Before the poor frightened mouse could answer, **CREEPELLA** grabbed one of his sleeves and **dragged** him out of the kitchen.

MYSTERIES AND FAINTING SPELLS

Before **BILLY** could argue, the sound of screeching music filled the air. The music ended on a **SHRILL** note that sounded like a crying cat.

"A violinist!" Shivereen exclaimed. "Let's find him!"

"Yes, let's find him!" Bitewing repeated. He did a **somersault** in the air.

"Let's find him," Creepella agreed. She looked at the map of the house, but it was full of eraser marks. She tossed it aside.

"But wh-why do we have to f-find him?" Billy asked, **terrified**. "Let's leave him in **PEACE** . . . whoever he is."

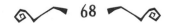

But Creepella was already heading down a looooooooooong, **dark** hallway.

They stopped in front of a door with a sign on it:

"Billy, open this door!" CREEPELLA demanded.

"B-but it says . . ."

"Don't let that **SCARE** you," she told him. "It's your house, after all!"

Billy gulped and opened the door to reveal . . . a room turned **upside down**! All of the **FURNITURE** was hanging from the ceiling!

Everything is t-t-turned upside down!

"It's n-n-not possible!" Billy stuttered in shock. "Everything's t-t-turned around."

Bitewing **ZIGZAGGED** in front of Billy. "**Ha-ha!** Tongue-tied again!"

Billy turned PALE. "M-my head is s-spinning," he said, and then he **fainted**.

"Poor thing," Shivereen said. "He didn't realize it's an illusion!"

Creepella pointed to the floor. "A typical magician's **TRICK**. MIRRORS reflect a drawing on the floor up onto the ceiling."

Bitewing giggled. "**And he fell for it!**"

Creepella looked down at Billy. "Maybe there are some **SMELLING SALTS** in the bathroom," she said. "Let's carry him there."

In the bathroom, they found an old brass **bathtub** filled with swampy water.

Shivereen dipped her paw into the tub.

"This water is
BOILING HOT!"
she shrieked.

"Another CLUE," Creepella
said. "This house is not
empty. Who would take a
bath here?"

"Him!" Bitewing giggled.
He found a bucketful of
FREEZING cold water
and dumped it
onto Billy's
head.
"Wake
up, Billy!"

But poor Billy had woken up just before the **FREEZING** water hit him. He stood up and ⸜*SLIPPED*⸝↗ on the wet floor. **Bam!** His snout hit the floor once more.

"Billy, you need to 🅂🅃🄾🄿 all this fainting," Creepella complained. "We have to go look for more **CLUES**!"

Creepella and the others left the bathroom.

Billy slowly sat up and rubbed his *bruised* whiskers. Suddenly, he realized he was **ALONE**.

"**DON'T LEAVE ME ALONE!**" he yelled. "**THIS H-HOUSE SCARES M-ME!**" Then he *ran* to catch up with Creepella, Shivereen, and Bitewing.

Silly Billy!

Oof . . . ouch!

THE BASEMENT

Billy ran down the hallway and entered a dark bedroom. The **BIGGEST** thing in the room was a large wooden wardrobe.

"Is anybody h-here?" he called out.

Nobody answered. Billy turned to leave when he heard a loud **squeak**. He looked back to see the doors of the wardrobe open slowly. A faint light **GLOWED** inside, giving him a glimpse of a **secret passage**.

Billy screamed,

"Aaaaaaaaaaaaahhhhhhhhhhhh!"

Creepella ran into the room. "Billy, why are you screaming?"

Bitewing flew in. "Seriously, you're going to wear out your voice with all that SCREAMING," he added.

Billy picked up an old **lantern** and shone it on the wardrobe. "It's a secret passage. Look!"

Wow! A secret passage!

Creepella raised her left eyebrow. "Hmm. It's a **DARK**, **DAMP**, **moldy** secret passage."

Bitewing flew down the passageway. "There are stairs leading down to the

BASEMENT!"

"Come quickly!" he called up to them. "It's a*m*a*z*i*n*g down here! Dark and damp and dusty! Just perfect!"

"Ooh! Come on, let's go," said Shivereen happily.

Billy refused to budge. "**NO! NO! NO!** I'm not going down there! There's nothing you can say to convince me! This time I'm not moving an inch!"

But Creepella pushed him into the wardrobe. The doors **slammed** shut behind them with a frightening bang. Billy had no choice — he had to follow her.

They walked **DOWN, DOWN, DOWN,** until they came to the entrance of a **maze** hidden in the darkness.

This way!

The Linen Closet

THE LINEN CLOSET

Bitewing led them through the *twisting*, turning **maze**.

"Let's go, Billy, *move* your **paws!**" Creepella scolded.

Billy followed reluctantly. Soon they came to a new door marked with a **strange** sign.

The door opened by itself with a sinister squeak.

SQUEEEEAK!

Suddenly, a puff of air as **cold** as a MUMMY'S breath blew out the lantern.

Now they could see a strange **GLOW** coming from the center of the room. The light came from underneath a large sheet covering a table and chairs.

Billy felt a shiver from the top of his ears to the **tip** of his tail.

"Wh-what's under the sh-sheet?" he stammered.

CREEPELLA walked up to the table. "Let's find out!" she shouted.

Billy ran to stop her as she grabbed the sheet, ready to pull it off the table. . . .

The Linen Closet...

...and its inhabitants!

Three cheers for the cook!

Yummy mummy! It's a soup right out of my nightmares!

The spider soup is marvelous!

Twelve Ghosts... Plus One?

"This is too much!" Billy shouted. "I'M FAINTING!"

His snout hit the floor once again. When he opened his eyes, he saw an incredible sight. Twelve ghosts were seated at the table, including a **dog**, a spider, and a mosquito! Each one of the ghosts glared at the intruders.

Creepella was so happy. Her search for ghosts was over at last!

"So nice to meet you," she said. "Can you please tell me who you are?"

"Y-yes," Billy stuttered. "Wh-who are you?"

A tall, thin ghost with his nose in the air was the first to speak.

"I am Simon Snootysnout, the butler of Squeakspeare Mansion," he said in a snobby voice. "It is my duty to inform you that we do not allow intruders of any kind here. You may not stay here. **LEAVE! DEPART! VAMOOSE! GET OUT! SHOO!**"

He floated around Creepella and the others, making Billy tremble with fright.

"How RUDE!" Creepella replied with a huff. "This is Billy's house, and we are his guests. You are the ones **HAUNTING** this house. Why don't *you* leave?"

"Show a little respect!" the butler replied. "We don't haunt this house. We **live** here. This is our home, whether your like it or not!"

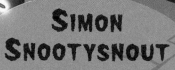

SIMON SNOOTYSNOUT
BUTLER

With centuries of experience, he has wisely taken care of Squeakspeare Mansion for as long as anyone can remember!

BOB WOODMOUSE
CARPENTER

He creates secret passageways and furniture with hidden compartments. (He built the passage in the wardrobe that leads to the basement.)

MISS DUSTMOP
HOUSEKEEPER

She is wonderful at mending cobwebs and polishing the green patches of mold on the walls.

HANK HAMMERAT
BLACKSMITH/LOCKSMITH

He makes links of clanking chains for ghosts. He'll make them out of solid gold by request.

BONNIE RAGU
COOK

She dreams of opening a gloomy restaurant for ghosts called The Last Meal. Her specialty is invisible meatballs.

TED TRIMMERTAIL
GARDENER

He is a master of making plants wither. Thanks to him, the mansion's garden is wild and full of thorny bushes.

Ned Needles

Tailor

He creates stylishly spooky
fashions for all the ghosts
in Mysterious Valley. He
specializes in silk sheets.

Dreamella Airhead

Maid

She always loses her glasses and
then finds them in the refrigerator,
or between the cushions in the
sofa, or in the secret passageway
in the wardrobe.

Gus Sip

Caretaker

He knows all the
gossip about the ghosts
in Mysterious Valley.

LEGGY
SPIDER ARTIST

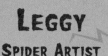

He weaves the strong
spiderwebs that decorate
Squeakspeare Mansion.

BUZZILLA
TOOTHLESS MOSQUITO

A music lover, she never
misses a concert. She
loves to buzz along
with the orchestra.

ARF
SLEEPWALKING DOG

At night, he digs holes in the
garden, searching for the bones
he's hidden. If only he could
remember where he buried them!

Billy turned white. "Maybe they're right," he whispered to Creepella. "We should go."

"Billy, don't be ridiculous!" Creepella said firmly. "It's your house, and you have the right to live here."

"But I don't want to live in a house full of ghosts," he replied, wringing his PAWS. "I just want a QUIET place where I can write my next book."

Simon Snootysnout froze. "Book!" he exclaimed. "Does that mean you're a writer?"

"Um . . . yes," Billy admitted.

The butler flew right in front of Billy's face. "A writer? A writer?"

"That's right," Billy repeated.

"A writer?" the butler asked again. "Really?"

"YES!" Billy shouted.

Snootysnout turned to the other ghosts.

"Did you hear that? He's a writer!"

The ghosts began to dance with joy around Billy. The poor mouse looked like he might FAINT again.

"We've been waiting for this day for a century!" Snootysnout cried.

Billy was CONFUSED. "What do you mean?"

The butler snapped his fingers. "Dreamella, bring all of our notes here!" he ordered.

The maid vanished. A moment later, she reappeared with a pile of PAPERS that went all the way up to the ceiling!

"These notes describe all of the records, events, SECRETS, and mysteries of Squeakspeare Mansion," the butler explained. He pointed at Billy dramatically. "We just need a famouse writer to transform them into a book of true TERROR!"

Finally, a writer!

Billy gulped. "Actually, I have other things to do," he said nervously.

"Don't **WORRY**, Mr. Writer. It won't take very long," replied Dreamella. "According to our calculations, you would only need to write about **754** volumes of **3,000** pages each. That should only take about **thirty years**!"

Billy gasped.

Simon Snootysnout had a proposition for him. "If you promise to work hard on the **BOOK**, we would let you stay in the house. As long as . . ."

"As long as?" Billy asked.

"As long as . . ." the butler repeated.

"As long as what?" Billy asked.

"As long as the **thirteenth ghost** agrees!" the butler finished.

"AND WHO IS THE THIRTEENTH GHOST?"

Creepella burst out impatiently.

Arf, the ghost dog, floated up to Creepella and wagged his tail.

"Arf will take you to the thirteenth ghost," Dreamella said. "**Follow him!**"

The dog **barked** and floated through the door at full speed.

Who is the thirteenth ghost?

THE THIRTEENTH GHOST

The dog left the linen closet and **ran** through the maze in the basement. He stopped in front of a **purple** door. Creepella opened it.

The walls of the round room were filled with bookcases. Each shelf was **STUFFED** with books.

"Brrr, it's **cold** in here!" Billy exclaimed with a shiver.

"I agree! I always say it's too cold in here," said a deep voice.

The voice came from a plump ghost with long, curly whiskers. He floated to a **RuSty** stove and smacked it with his walking stick.

"This old **WRECK** of a stove doesn't work properly," he complained. "Hank! Come quickly!"

The blacksmith ghost appeared in the room. "Still having problems with the stove, Mr. William?" he asked.

Billy gasped. "William? You're **WiLLiaM SQueaKSPeaRe**? My great-great-great-uncle William?" he asked in surprise.

The ghost turned around and **smiled**. "Then you must be my great-great-great-nephew Billy! Well, **tickle** my whiskers, what a wonderful surprise! Come here and give me a **hug**."

Billy threw his arms around the ghost . . . and then **FELL** snoutfirst onto the floor.

William laughed. "Sorry, I forgot. We can't touch!"

Creepella cleared her throat. "I'm sorry to interrupt your **family reunion**, but I have some interviews to do!" she snapped.

"Interviews?" William asked. "Ah, I remember those. I was interviewed many

What a surprise!

times after I won the **Mysterious Valley Comedy Contest**. Did you know that I won the famous Laugh Your Tail Off award seventeen years in a row?"

"Fantastic!" Creepella exclaimed. "If you'd like to tell some jokes, I'll include them in the article I'm writing about ghosts."

"Of course!" William replied. "My GHOULISH jokes are guaranteed to make your whiskers twitch!"

Then he winked at Billy. "What a **lovely** mouse you've chosen for a girlfriend, nephew. When are you getting married?"

Billy looked more AFRAID than when he had seen the ghosts. "M-m-married?"

Creepella put her paw on his shoulder. "Don't be such a **Stick-iN-the-MUD**, Billy," she said. "I think we make a good couple. What do you think, Shivereen?"

Shivereen got a *dreamy* look on her face. "You're a couple from my **DEEPEST** nightmares," she replied. "My favorite aunt and the writer who's dearest to my heart!"

"Bouncing bookmarks! I don't want to get married!" Billy squealed.

"But you must," insisted William. "At your age you're almost too moldy for MARRIAGE."

Bitewing zipped between them. "CREEPELLA VON CACKLEFUR married to a scaredy-mouse writer of romance novels. Hee hee hee! That's a joke," he said gleefully.

"I know better jokes than that," William boasted. "Listen to these!"

WILLIAM SQUEAKSPEARE'S GHOULISH JOKES

HA HA HA

Why do dragons sleep during the day?

So they can fight Knights!

HA HA HA

Why did the skeleton stay home from the dance?

Because he had no-body to go with!

Where do ghosts like to go swimming?

In the Dead Sea

HA HA HA

CLEANING AT MIDNIGHT

Creepella wrote down Great-great-great-uncle William Squeakspeare's **jokes**. Then she interviewed all twelve of the other **ghosts** in the house.

"Finally, I have enough material for my article!" she said happily.

"Let's return to Cacklefur Castle! You must start writing right away!" Bitewing shrieked.

Meanwhile, Billy brought all of his luggage into the house.

First he put his clothes in a bedroom. Then he brought his books to the study. But there was no room for them. It was filled to the brim with rolls of paper, notepads, and STACKS AND STACKS of notebooks.

The butler and maid appeared behind him.

"Look!" cried Snootysnout, startling Billy. "These are all the NOTES you'll need to write the introduction to the book."

"Introduction?" Billy wondered.

"Of course," said Dreamella. "Let us know when you've finished, and we'll bring you the rest."

Billy was starting to get a BAD feeling. "The rest?"

"Why, these notes are just a start," Dreamella told him. "In the basement there are 389 bookshelves full of notes, 1,755

chests full of notebooks, and **5,016** rolls of paper! Aren't you excited?"

Billy **FAINTED** on top of a pile of paper. That's where Creepella found him.

"You've fainted again?" she asked with a sigh.

William shook his head. "Ah, these young mice today. As **soft** as cream cheese!"

When he came to, Billy decided he might as well help the ghosts **write** the history of Squeakspeare Mansion. After all, he was happy to live in his family home. There was just one small **PROBLEM**. He soon discovered that the thirteen ghosts liked to clean the house . . . at **MIDNIGHT**!

DONG! DONG! DONG!
Good-bye, dust!
Hammer here, hammer there!
Now where did I leave that?
Nice and tidy!
Arf! Arf!

A New Writer!

Creepella's article was published in the next issue of **THE SHIVERY NEWS**. It was such a

success that she decided to write a book. She wrote all about her adventure at Squeakspeare Mansion.

"**I'M FINISHED!**" she cried, as she typed her last line. "Now it's time for me to **CONQUER** the world of books!"

"You have to find someone to publish it first," Bitewing pointed out.

"Of course!" Creepella said. "And I have just the right rodent in mind. Are you ready to FLUTTER all the way to New Mouse City?"

"Hee hee hee!" Bitewing laughed as he flapped around her desk. "I get it! You're talking about *Geronimo Stilton*. But are you sure he's the right one? He's a big scaredy-mouse!"

"Don't worry," Creepella said confidently. "I'm sure that even he won't be able to resist my CHILLING story. It's a truly THRILLING tale!"

THE END

A THRILLING BESTSELLER!

Can you guess? The book was a colossal SUCCESS! The publisher (that's me, *Geronimo Stilton*) was flooded with **FAN MAIL**. The phone rang all the time. Everyone asked the same question:

"When is Creepella's next book coming out?"

What great pictures!   They're fantastic!

I didn't know how to answer. Then my cell phone rang, and it was CREEPELLA VON CACKLEFUR!

"So, my dear, did you like the story?" she squealed.

I had to admit that even I had enjoyed her scary story.

"Congratulations, CREEPELLA!" I told her. "It's a truly THRILLING bestseller!"

If you liked this book, be sure to check out Creepella's next adventure!

MEET ME IN HORRORWOOD

Something is wrong with Gorgo, the monster in the moat of Cacklefur Castle! Creepella discovers that he is lovesick for the monster Blobbina, who also happens to be a famous movie star. But when Creepella writes Blobbina a love letter from Gorgo, she finds out Blobbina has disappeared! Creepella and Billy Squeakspeare head to Horrorwood to search for the missing Blobbina. Will they ever find her?

And don't miss any of my other fabumouse adventures!

#1 Lost Treasure of the Emerald Eye

#2 The Curse of the Cheese Pyramid

#3 Cat and Mouse in a Haunted House

#4 I'm Too Fond of My Fur!

#5 Four Mice Deep in the Jungle

#6 Paws Off, Cheddarface!

#7 Red Pizzas for a Blue Count

#8 Attack of the Bandit Cats

#9 A Fabumouse Vacation for Geronimo

#10 All Because of a Cup of Coffee

#11 It's Halloween, You 'Fraidy Mouse!

#12 Merry Christmas, Geronimo!

#13 The Phantom of the Subway

#14 The Temple of the Ruby of Fire

#15 The Mona Mousa Code

#16 A Cheese-Colored Camper

#17 Watch Your Whiskers, Stilton!

#18 Shipwreck on the Pirate Islands

#19 My Name Is Stilton, Geronimo Stilton

#20 Surf's Up, Geronimo!

#21 The Wild, Wild West

#22 The Secret of Cacklefur Castle

A Christmas Tale

#23 Valentine's Day Disaster

#24 Field Trip to Niagara Falls

#25 The Search for Sunken Treasure

#26 The Mummy with No Name

#27 The Christmas Toy Factory

#28 Wedding Crasher

#29 Down and Out Down Under

#30 The Mouse Island Marathon

#31 The Mysterious Cheese Thief

Christmas Catastrophe

#32 Valley of the Giant Skeletons

#33 Geronimo and the Gold Medal Mystery

#34 Geronimo Stilton, Secret Agent

#35 A Very Merry Christmas

#36 Geronimo's Valentine

#37 The Race Across America

#38 A Fabumouse School Adventure

#39 Singing Sensation

#40 The Karate Mouse

#41 Mighty Mount Kilimanjaro

#42 The Peculiar Pumpkin Thief

#43 I'm Not a Supermouse!

#44 The Giant Diamond Robbery

#45 Save the White Whale!

#46 The Haunted Castle

And coming soon!

#47 Run for the Hills, Geronimo!

1. Mountains of the Mangy Yeti
2. Cacklefur Castle
3. Angry Walnut Tree
4. Rattenbaum Palace
5. Rancidrat River
6. Bridge of Shaky Steps
7. Squeakspeare Mansion
8. Slimy Swamp
9. Ogre Highway
10. Gloomeria
11. Shivery Arts Academy
12. Horrorwood Studios

1. Oozing moat

2. Drawbridge

3. Grand entrance

4. Moldy basement

5. Patio, with a view of the moat

6. Dusty library

7. Room for unwanted guests

8. Mummy room

9. Watchtower

10. Creaking staircase

11. Banquet room

12. Garage (for antique hearses)

13. Bewitched tower

14. Garden of carnivorous plants

15. Stinky kitchen

16. Crocodile pool and piranha tank

17. Creepella's room

18. Tower of musky tarantulas

19. Bitewing's tower (with antique contraptions)

DEAR MOUSE FRIENDS, GOOD-BYE UNTIL THE NEXT BOOK!